BLACKOUT

For Blitz Girl and Sailor Boy

While the events described and some of the characters in
this book may be based on actual historical events and real people,
Jimmy Wilson is a fictional character, created by the author,
and his story is a work of fiction.

Scholastic Children's Books,
Euston House, 24 Eversholt Street,
London NW1 1DB, UK

A division of Scholastic Ltd
London ~ New York ~ Toronto ~ Sydney ~ Auckland
Mexico City ~ New Delhi ~ Hong Kong

First published in the UK by Scholastic Ltd, 2019

ISBN 978 1407 19329 8

Text © Tony Bradman, 2019
Cover artwork © Two Dots

Printed and bound by
CPI Group (UK) Ltd, Croydon, CR0 4YY

2 4 6 8 10 9 7 5 3 1

CANCELLED

BLACKOUT

SCHOLASTIC

CHAPTER

I knew I was in trouble as soon as I heard Mum's key in the front door. At that moment I was in the sitting room of our flat reading a comic. It was an old *Beano* I'd got from my mate Harry Jones in a swap at school. He'd wanted half my trading cards, but I didn't really mind. There's nothing like losing yourself in a comic and this was a particularly good issue. The Lord Snooty story was great and there were also some funny cartoons about Hitler and the Nazis.

But I should have been in the kitchen peeling

potatoes, not just enjoying myself. Mum was at work all day, so she needed plenty of help from me and my little sister Mavis. We each had a list of jobs to do and one of mine was to make sure things were ready for our dinner to be cooked when Mum came home in the evening. I should have had those spuds peeled and in a pan on the cooker ages ago.

There wasn't a second to lose. I stuffed the comic behind a cushion, jumped out of the armchair, and made a quick dash across the hall to the kitchen. By the time Mum was inside the flat I was standing at the sink, whistling cheerily as I peeled potatoes like mad. I heard Mum in the hall and then I sensed her looming in the kitchen doorway behind me. I turned and gave her a winning smile.

"Oh, hello Mum!" I said, trying to look surprised. "I didn't hear you come in."

"He's lying, Mum!" said Mavis. My sister had appeared and was peeking round her. "He was in the sitting room reading a comic until he heard your key in the door."

"Hey, shut up, Mavis!" I said. "You shouldn't have been spying on me!"

"See? He admits it!" said Mavis, smirking. I stuck my tongue out at her.

"That's enough, you two," said Mum with a deep sigh. "Be a good boy, Jimmy, and put the kettle on. It's been a long day and I could really do with a cup of tea."

Mum sat down at the table, which filled most of the kitchen, and kicked off her shoes. I could hear the tiredness in her voice and that made me feel guilty. But then everyone was tired in those days, kids as well as grown-ups. It was early December 1943, and we'd been through four years of total war with Nazi Germany – four years of food rationing, bad news and bombs. There was no doubt that Hitler was a bad man and we had to beat him. But it seemed to be taking a very long time.

We'd moved into Wellington Mansions in 1939, pretty soon after the Council built it. The block was near the Waterloo Road, not far from Waterloo station. Before that we'd been in a flat over a butcher's shop in Camberwell. The new flat was much nicer, with two bedrooms, a sitting room and a bathroom with a toilet. Now that was a real luxury – the toilet for our first flat was outside in the backyard. We were on the third floor, so there weren't lots of stairs, which was good when you had shopping or coal to carry up. The front doors on each floor looked down into the courtyard. It was mostly families that lived in the block, and none of us had a lot of money. But that didn't matter – it was a great place to live.

Mum always said that 1939 had been a very good year for us. She and Dad had grown up in poor families and times had been tough when they were young. Mum's dad was killed in the First World War and her mum had died of consumption later on. Dad's parents had died in the 1920s and he had lived in an orphanage for a while. Neither of them had any brothers or sisters – maybe that's why they got on so well. In any case, they had both worked hard after they got married and eventually they'd begun to do all right. Dad trained to be a motor mechanic and Mum as a typist.

I was six in 1939, Mavis was three, and we were a very happy family. There was a framed picture on the mantlepiece of the four of us that was taken on a day at the seaside in Margate before the war started.

Even though the photo was black and white, I remember how Mum looked like a film star in her blue summer frock, her blonde hair shining in the sunlight. Dad was beside her, in a white shirt, his arm round her shoulders. He's tall and dark-haired and Mum says I look like him – Mavis and Mum are both fair-haired. Mavis and me were standing in front of them, holding hands and grinning. I was wearing a short-sleeved shirt and a pair of shorts, and Mavis had on a yellow dress. Me and Mavis might argue sometimes, but we get on fine, really.

Then rotten old Hitler decided to start a war and everything changed.

I made Mum a cup of tea and finished peeling the potatoes. I put them on to boil and got the frying pan out so Mum could cook the liver and onions she'd bought. Soon the three of us were sitting at the little table eating our dinner. For afters we ate tinned pears with evaporated milk, then I volunteered to do the washing up on my own. I made Mum go and put her feet up in the sitting room with Mavis.

"You *are* a good boy, Jimmy Wilson," Mum said when I'd finished. "Now come and sit down with us.

Let's hope there's something funny on the wireless tonight."

The three of us sat squashed together on the settee, Mum in the middle. That's how you'd have found us most nights, especially in the winter. We only ever had enough coal to keep the fire going for a couple of hours in the evening, so we huddled close for warmth. But I think we all felt safer that way too. For just a while we could forget that the world outside was cold and dark and full of terrible things going on.

We had been through some pretty bad stuff ourselves. When the war began in September 1939 I was evacuated with my school – Mum and Dad kept Mavis at home because she was so young. I ended up on a farm in Devon, feeling frightened and homesick, but I didn't stay there long. London wasn't bombed after all and half the kids who had been evacuated ended up back home before the first Christmas of the war. I was home by October – Mum soon told the school she couldn't see the point of me being evacuated. After that, she swore she would never, ever send me away again. She said that we would stay together, whatever happened.

Dad was gone by the time I got home – he had been called up. He had expected to go into the Army because he was a mechanic, maybe the Royal Engineers, but they put him in the Royal Navy instead. It seemed barmy to me, but according to Mum, Dad didn't mind. He was just keen 'to do his bit' in the war, as people said. Mum had put a brave face on it, although I knew she worried about him all the time. So did I.

Dad was posted as an Ordinary Seaman to the destroyer HMS *Defiant*. He wrote us letters, but he wasn't allowed to say where the ship was or what it was doing and he only came home on leave twice a year.

Later, the newspapers called those early months the 'Phoney War' because nothing much happened – it was as if neither side wanted to upset the other. But the truth was that the Germans were just fooling us. They suddenly launched a massive attack and the war became very real. We should have expected it, I suppose. Hitler had a habit of telling lies and breaking the rules.

I was only seven in 1940, but I remember those

dark days – the little ships getting our soldiers off the beaches at Dunkirk, the fall of France – and then the Blitz. The German air force, the *Luftwaffe*, dropped bombs on London every night for months. After a while we didn't even bother to wait for the howl of the warning siren. As soon as the sun went down Mum took us to the Underground station at Waterloo and we waited out the night with everyone else.

It was terrifying. We could hear the bombs even though we were underground. They whistled as they fell and the floor shook when they went off – it felt like an angry giant was stamping through the city. When the steady drone of the 'all clear' signal sounded and we came up, the streets were full of rubble, broken glass and shrapnel, and everywhere smelt smoky because of the fires. Lots of people were wounded or killed and loads of homes were flattened. People who were 'bombed out' had to be rehoused, sometimes miles from where they lived before.

We survived though, and the RAF, our very own Royal Air Force, won what came to be called the Battle of Britain – they defended the skies and shot down an awful lot of Nazi planes. The Germans eventually stopped bombing London in the spring of 1941, not long before Hitler decided to invade Russia. As Mum said, he had bigger fish to fry now. I felt sorry for the Russians, but I was also glad the Germans were leaving us alone, even if it was only for a while. The war dragged on and it began to look like Hitler might even win. The Russians didn't seem able to stop his forces, the *Wehrmacht*.

It got so bad that Mum didn't want to listen to the news on the wireless any more. We were all in a deep gloom – the Germans were advancing everywhere. But in the last year there had been a change. We managed to beat the Germans at El Alamein in North Africa and the Russians beat them in a gigantic battle at Stalingrad. The Americans, or 'Yanks' as we called them, had been in the war on our side since the end of 1941 and American soldiers had at last begun to arrive over here – it sometimes seemed London was full of them.

With things beginning to look up, Mum was happy to listen to the news again. We had a good wireless set – Dad bought it before the war. It had a brown wooden case and the names of foreign radio stations in lights on the front. In the evenings, there was a variety show, with a singer and comedians, which was a lot of fun. The news came on right after that finished. Soon we were listening to a familiar posh voice.

"This is the Nine O'Clock News on the BBC and this is Alvar Liddell reading it..."

The main report was about a huge battle for the city of Kiev in the Ukraine – the Russians had finally recaptured it from the Germans. Alvar Liddell was just about to move on to the next report, but we all heard a noise and stopped listening, our eyes wide. We heard the key in the front door and then footsteps crossed the hall, approaching the sitting room. The door slowly opened and Dad walked in! He stood there in his duffel coat and his Navy cap, a kitbag slung over his shoulder.

"Well, this is a fine welcome and no mistake!" he said, smiling. "Isn't anyone going to give me a hug? Although at the moment I'd settle for a nice cup of tea."

We jumped up and hugged him as hard as we could. Mum started crying, that set Mavis off and

I nearly started blubbing too. But then we quickly settled down.

"Oh, George, why didn't you let us know that you were coming home?" said Mum.

"Well I only found out myself yesterday, Kath. The *Defiant* is going into dry dock up North for a refit, so they let us all have leave. I'll be at home for Christmas!"

It was a smashing end to the year – which was just as well, really. The next year turned out to be the worst one of our lives.

CHAPTER

2

We stayed up talking late that night, which meant we were a bit slow getting out of bed in the morning. Mavis and me were supposed to go to school, but I asked Mum if we could stay at home instead. We both wanted to spend the day with Dad.

"Certainly not! Don't you know there's a war on?" Mum said with a frown. Nobody needed to be reminded of that. But funnily enough, it was something grown-ups said all the time, usually when they wanted to stop you having fun. "A fine pickle the country would be in if everyone just stopped at home whenever they felt like it," Mum added. "You might as well invite the Germans in and make them tea."

We were sitting in the kitchen having breakfast. Not that there was much to eat, only toast with a thin scrape of marmalade on it. I couldn't remember the last time I'd seen an egg or a rasher of bacon. I tried not to think about food, but it was hard. The longer the war went on, the less there was for everyone. Hitler had been getting his submarines – his U-boats – to sink the ships bringing us food across the sea.

Mind you, we knew now that Dad and his shipmates had been doing their best to stop that happening. He told us HMS *Defiant* had mostly been in the North Atlantic, guarding the great convoys of merchant ships coming to us from America – they were under constant attack. HMS *Defiant* had also been up in the Arctic, protecting the ships taking supplies to the Russians through icy seas and terrible storms.

It sounded awful. Dad told us that sometimes the ship's decks were covered in sheets of ice and huge icicles hung from the barrels of the guns.

The sailors had to chip the ice off every day. If they didn't, it could make the ship top-heavy and a big wave might turn it right over. Dad said that wasn't ever going to happen, but I wished he hadn't mentioned it. Up until then I had just worried about German planes and submarines attacking him. Now I had the weather to worry about as well.

"Oh go on, Mum, be a sport!" I said. "Tell her to let us stay at home, Dad."

"Sorry, son," said Dad, shrugging. "I agree with your mum. We all have to do our bit in the war and your job is going to school. Education is very important."

Dad was right, I suppose, but I didn't think we were getting much of an education. Our school – St Edmund's – never really recovered from being evacuated when the war began. Half the kids didn't come back and most of the teachers had stayed with them or been called up. The same was true for plenty of other schools in London and quite a few were closed during the worst months of the Blitz – some were even damaged in the bombing.

Our headmaster Mr Jackson managed to keep our

school open. But there were only two classes, with over forty kids in each. Mavis was in the younger class and her teacher was young Mrs Peters, who was lovely. Us bigger kids had to put up with mean old Mrs Reynolds. She had retired just before the war and only came back to help out. We wished she hadn't bothered – she often spent the day telling us off.

I hadn't said any of that to Mum, though. I reckoned she had more than enough on her plate without me complaining about school. Her job was quite important – she worked as a typist at the Ministry of Labour in Whitehall, on the other side of the river. She said it was where the government organised the workers for all the vital industries. The three of us usually left together in the mornings. Mum walked Mavis and me to school and then she went on to catch the bus outside Waterloo station.

"And remember, Jimmy, you don't have to collect your sister from Marge's this afternoon," said Mum when we were about to leave. "Your dad will do that."

The two classes at our school finished at different times, the younger kids getting out at two-thirty, us older kids at quarter to four. Mum hated the idea of

Mavis walking home alone, but luckily there was someone who could help, Mum's friend Marge. Mavis likes Marge and so do I – we call her Auntie Marge. Her husband Alf was with the Eighth Army in North Africa, and now they were fighting in Italy. Alf and Marge didn't have any kids yet, and she worked in a factory in Deptford that made ammunition for the army. She did shifts and she could always arrange things to look after Mavis and me for Mum. Mum usually comes home at about six thirty, I collect Mavis from Auntie Marge's after school, and then we walk home together.

"See you later, kids," said Dad, smiling at us. "I'm sure the day will fly past."

It didn't. If anything it seemed to crawl more slowly than ever. Mrs Reynolds was very grumpy and she made us do our times tables over and over again. The whole class had to chant them together and it was really boring. I couldn't wait for the day to finish. When the bell went at quarter to four, I shot out of school and ran home as quickly as I could.

It was a dark December evening and the streets were almost pitch black because of the blackout. I had my torch with me, but I could have made the journey home with my eyes closed. I suppose we'd got used to there not being any lights in the streets after dark – the blackout rule had come in at the beginning of the war. It made sense, of course. Leaving the lights on would have made it easy for the *Luftwaffe* to see where to drop their bombs. But I remembered how things had been before the war, the street lamps glowing, the windows of shops and houses full of bright lights. Now special Air Raid Precaution wardens patrolled all the streets to check that everybody was sticking to the rule. Sometimes you'd hear an ARP warden shout, "Put that bloomin' light out!"

I'd also got used to the flat being cold and dark when Mavis and I came home after school, but tonight it was warm and bright. Dad had put up the blackout blinds so the lights were on and he had also made up the fire. Two big logs were merrily burning away in the grate and he'd been down to the courtyard to fill the coal scuttle for the evening.

"Blimey, where did you get the logs?" I asked. "We haven't had any for ages!"

"A bloke had a heap of them down at the market in

Lower Marsh," Dad said. "It was lucky I spotted him – I swear he sold the lot in about two minutes flat."

"That's not all," Mavis said excitedly. "We're having chops for dinner!"

I could hardly believe it, but it was true. Dad had managed to find probably the only pork chops in London. Apparently Ernie, the man who owned the butchers we used to live over, owed Dad a favour. The chops were actually more fat than meat, but we ate them with mashed potato and some spinach and they tasted good to me. Although Mum moaned a bit – she hates the idea of doing anything dodgy.

"Oh, George, I do wish you hadn't got them from Ernie," she said. "Just the other day someone was telling me he's well known for selling under the counter."

That's what people say when they accuse a shopkeeper of selling stuff they shouldn't to make extra money for themselves, but if you've got enough money you can buy plenty you're not supposed to. Mum reckons that's not fair, so she won't buy anything on the 'Black Market', as it's often called.

"Ernie's all right," said Dad. "He only does that

kind of thing for his old mates. Besides, we're not doing it all the time. I don't see the harm in it myself."

Mum gave him a look, but she didn't make any more fuss. Like Mavis and me, she was happy to have Dad back and I could tell she didn't want to spoil things. I have to say I agreed with Dad. It didn't seem like that much of a big deal to me.

We had such a good time over the next two weeks. I'd forgotten what a lot of fun Dad could be. He played with Mavis and he took me to the park so we could have a kickabout with a football. He also took me with him to Camberwell market to buy our Christmas tree. Mum and Mavis made decorations for the tree and the flat. They cut up old magazines to make paper chains and they looked great.

For Christmas dinner we had a plump rabbit, supplied by Ernie the butcher, of course – Mum didn't say a word. There were potatoes too, and carrots and turnips. Mum had even managed to make a proper Christmas pudding and she hid a couple of sixpences in it. I don't know how, but Mum made sure Mavis and me found a sixpence each.

That night we played Charades, and then we

listened to the wireless. There was a good variety show on and the news wasn't too grim. It almost felt like old times with us all being together again. I think we enjoyed it more because we knew it couldn't last. Boxing Day was fun too, but the next morning a telegram arrived for Dad. He was being recalled to the *Defiant* and had to leave immediately.

Mum and Mavis cried again and I did as well this time. I didn't want Dad to go. There had been a report on the news about a sea-battle north of Norway. A Royal Navy force including the battleship *Duke of York* and the cruisers *Belfast*, *Norfolk* and *Sheffield* had attacked and sunk the German battleship *Scharnhorst*. It was a victory for us, but it only made me worry about what Dad might have to face when he went back to sea. What if HMS *Defiant* got involved in a big battle like that?

"I'll be fine, Jimmy," said Dad when he was getting ready to go. We were together in Mum and Dad's bedroom, Dad packing away his stuff in his kitbag. Mum and Mavis were in the hall putting on their coats. "And I don't want you worrying about me all the time," Dad continued. "You're the man of the house while I'm away and I'm relying on you to keep your mind focused on taking care of your mum and sister."

He was smiling when he said it and he ruffled my hair, so I knew he was more than half joking. I also knew Mum could look after herself as well as me and Mavis. After all, that's what she'd been doing all the time Dad had been away. But still, it did feel as if he was giving me a special job and I took him seriously.

"You can count on me, Dad," I said. "I promise I won't let you down."

Little did I know that those words would come back to haunt me.

CHAPTER

Dad's orders said he was to go to the big naval base at Portsmouth on the south coast – the *Defiant* would head there with some of the crew once her refit was finished. It was lucky as trains to Portsmouth departed from Waterloo, so it meant we could see Dad off at the station. There were more tears, of course. The three of us waved to Dad as the train pulled out and we kept waving till we couldn't see him any more.

That was in early January, a few days into 1944. Mum did her best to keep us all cheerful, but we were pretty glum – things weren't the same without Dad around. School was boring, evenings at home were boring, the news was boring. The Russian advance on the Eastern Front had slowed and our lads were struggling to push the Germans back in Italy. At this rate I thought the war might carry on for years.

In fact there was only one thing that could really make me smile – my visits to the pictures. I've loved the pictures ever since Mum and Dad took me to see my first film just before the war. It was *Snow White and the Seven Dwarfs* and everything about it was wonderful – the colours up on the screen, the music, the characters. There was something magical about sitting in the dark, completely gripped by the story.

In the last year I'd got into the habit of going to the pictures with my friends from school, especially Harry. We usually met on Saturday afternoons at the Regal, our local picture house – it's much nicer than any of the other cinemas near us. Dad called them 'the flea-pits' – they were definitely a bit old and grubby. The Regal was only built in the 1930s and it still looked brand new, even after four hard years of war.

Mum didn't mind – she thinks it's a good idea for me to get out of the flat on Saturdays. That's the day she does the cleaning and washing – she says she gets on much better if I'm not under her feet or bickering with Mavis because I'm bored. But a couple of weeks after Dad went back to his ship, Mum announced at dinner one Friday evening that she had been asked to go into the office the next day.

"I could do without it, but I don't feel I can say no," she said, sighing. "We're so busy at the moment, and as Mr Churchill says, we all have to make sacrifices to back the war effort. And I suppose the overtime money will come in handy too."

I stopped eating and stared at her, a piece of Spam dangling from my fork. Mr Churchill is our Prime Minister, the leader of our government. His first name is Winston, but some people call him 'Winnie'. He took over in the dark days of 1940, and Mum says if it hadn't been for him we would probably have surrendered. He often talked on the wireless to the nation and we all thought he was great. But I didn't want to give up a trip to the pictures, not even for good old Winnie.

"Oh no," I moaned. "Does that mean I'll have to stay in to look after Mavis?"

"Certainly not," Mavis snapped. "I can look after myself, can't I, Mum?"

"Relax, the pair of you," said Mum. "Mavis, I've asked Marge if she'll have you for the day. I think you'll enjoy that more than being stuck at home arguing with your brother. So you *can* go to the pictures, Jimmy. You'll have to collect your sister and bring her back, though. Marge will expect you at six o'clock. Don't be late."

"I won't be, Mum," I said with a big smile. "Cross my heart and hope to die."

"Don't say things like that, Jimmy, you're tempting fate!" Mum shuddered as if she was suddenly cold. She crossed her fingers on both hands and reached out to touch the wood of the kitchen table. "None of us will be safe till this war is over."

"Sorry, Mum," I said, and popped the bit of Spam into my mouth. Mum often came out with gloomy stuff like that.

The next morning I volunteered to take Mavis to Marge's and we all set off early together. The weather had turned a bit milder, but Mum still made sure we were wearing our winter coats. I had nearly outgrown mine, but new coats were very hard to come by. Mum had also knitted gloves for us, using the wool from an old jumper. She caught her bus at Waterloo and Mavis and I carried on to Marge's.

"Coming in for a cup of tea, Jimmy?" Marge said when she opened the door of her place in Dodson Street. It's in a terrace of small houses. Marge is little and round, with dark frizzy hair and a smiley face and she's full of fun and laughter. Mum and her have been best friends since they were kids, so I've known her my whole life. "Why don't you stay?" Marge added. "We could have a lovely day together!"

"Er, no thanks, Marge," I said. I liked Marge, but I liked the idea of having the morning to myself much more. "Actually, I've got a lot of things planned."

"Ooh, hark at your big brother, Mavis!" she said, and laughed. "Excuse me for asking! Well, I suppose us girls can just about survive without you."

"You'll have to," I said. "There *is* a war on, you know – see you later."

"Cheeky!" said Marge, and pretended to cuff me

round the ear. But she was smiling as she did it and I smiled back as I ducked. Then I walked off and Mavis went into the house. Marge stood there, waving until I turned the corner. I remember so clearly the way she looked at that moment, framed in the doorway of her small house.

I went home so I could enjoy reading my comics without being interrupted – I'd got a few more in swaps at school. Then I read the *Just William* book Mum and Dad had bought me for Christmas. Those stories always made me laugh – William and his friends call themselves 'The Outlaws' and they get up to all sorts of mischief.

I felt bored after a while, though, and I decided to go out even though I didn't have to meet my mates till two o'clock. Mum had given me a couple of shillings for the day. A ticket for the pictures would cost me sixpence, but I would still have enough to buy a bag of chips before I went in. I was also going to try and buy some sweets. They were rationed too, but big shops like Woolworth's occasionally got a special delivery.

As usual, Waterloo station and the streets around it were busy. There weren't many cars, of course – petrol was rationed as well – but there were plenty of buses. Lots of people were arriving at the station or coming out of it, many of them in uniform. It was fascinating to watch them – half the world seemed to be coming together to fight rotten old Hitler and his Nazis. I saw British soldiers, sailors and airmen, but also Yanks, Canadians, Aussies, Kiwis, Indians, Frenchmen, Danes, Czechs, Poles and loads more. I saw women in uniform as well, ATS girls, Wrens and WAAFs. I wondered if any of the British sailors might know my dad, but I was too shy to ask. So I hung about, bought a bag of chips, and then I went to Woolworth's. But surprise, surprise, they didn't have any sweets.

Harry was waiting outside the Regal's glass doors when I got there. I spotted him straightaway, even though he was surrounded by the usual crowd waiting for the doors to open. You can't really miss him – he's tall, gangly and ginger.

"All right, Jimmy?" he said, grinning. "Looks like it's just you and me – none of the others have turned up. More fool them, I reckon. There's some good stuff on today."

"That's brilliant," I said. The doors opened at

'exactly two o'clock and the whole crowd surged forward. "Come on, let's get our tickets before they all go."

We pushed into the lobby, queued up, handed over our sixpences and then headed to the stalls. We got a couple of seats in the front row, right underneath the screen. I liked being up close – sometimes it felt as if you were almost inside the film.

The lights went down at last and the programme started. There was always a short film from the Ministry of Information about things like growing vegetables ('Dig for Victory'), or not revealing any secrets to German spies, like where your soldier husband had been posted ('Careless Talk Costs Lives'). They could be quite funny, but we'd seen them all before so they weren't really telling us anything new.

Next was the 'B' picture. It was a Western, with Tom Mix, so there were endless chases on horseback and gunfights between cowboys – I quite like Westerns, but Harry absolutely loves them. 'B' pictures weren't as long as the main feature and they were always followed by a newsreel. That was like the news on the wireless, only with moving pictures as well as someone talking.

That day it was the usual mix of reports from home and abroad, most of them to do with the war. We always booed whenever rotten old Hitler or his cronies appeared and the grown-ups yelled out rude words. But that day there was a report about Arctic convoys, with film shot on our warships. Of course I was utterly gripped and I scanned the faces of the sailors on the screen in case one of them was Dad.

I didn't see him, though, and the newsreel was soon over. Next came the main feature, a Hollywood thriller about a private detective. I usually loved Hollywood movies, but I just wanted this one to end. Once it was over I could stay in my seat and watch the whole programme over again – you didn't have to buy another ticket. I wanted to see the newsreel again – maybe I'd missed Dad. Harry stayed too.

But then suddenly, not long after the newsreel came on once more, I remembered I was supposed to collect Mavis from Marge's at six o'clock! I had no idea what the time was – I didn't have a watch. I jumped up and ran out and Harry followed me.

There was a clock in the lobby. My heart sank when I saw that it was half-past six and it was dark outside. It would take me ages to get to Marge's place, even if I ran like the clappers. I had a feeling Mum wasn't going to be very pleased with me.

"What's up, Jimmy?" said Harry. "Where are you off to in such a hurry?"

"I've got to collect my sister," I said as we stepped outside. "And I'm—"

A terrible noise drowned out the rest of what I was going to say. It was a sound we hadn't heard for quite a while, but one that instantly made my blood turn cold – the dreaded howling of the air raid sirens. We both looked up at the night sky.

The *Luftwaffe* was coming.

CHAPTER

It was Saturday evening and the street was busy with people. Everyone stood still at the howling of the sirens as if they couldn't believe what they were hearing. The searchlights came on all over London, the familiar giant beams of light crisscrossing as they probed the dark night sky. Then we heard another sound, the deep throbbing of aircraft engines, and suddenly everyone started moving *very* quickly.

"Crikey, I didn't think I'd hear that again!" Harry muttered. "I'd better be off home. Come with me,

Jimmy, we've still got the Anderson shelter in our backyard."

"No, I can't," I said. "I think I'd better go home too. See you, Harry."

He nodded, and we ran off in different directions. I headed up the Waterloo Road – I'd decided that the best thing would be to make for our flat. Mum would probably have gone round to Marge's and brought Mavis home herself when she discovered I hadn't done it. At least that was what I was hoping. Once we were together we could go to the Tube station and take shelter underground till after the raid.

I put on a burst of speed, weaving through the people hurrying along the pavement. After a while I came to a corner where a small crowd had gathered outside a Public Shelter. There were quite a few of those, usually in cellars or basements that had been made deeper and stronger. This one was beneath a tall old house, the entrance to the shelter was a side door surrounded by lots of sandbags. An ARP warden stood by the door, counting the people as they ducked inside. I kept running, but he spotted me.

"Hey, you!" he shouted, grabbing my arm. He was

old and thin in his dark uniform and his tin helmet was far too big for him, but his bony fingers were like an iron clamp. "Can't you hear the sirens? You need to get in here sharpish, my lad."

"Let go of me!" I said. "I have to go home, to my mum and sister!"

"Too late for that," he said, pulling me towards the doorway. Everyone else had gone in. "If they've any sense they'll be in a shelter themselves by now."

Just then the sirens stopped and the throbbing of the engines grew much louder. Me and the warden both looked up and I could see the German planes, their small, deadly shapes caught in the searchlight beams. There were loud bangs too, the anti-aircraft guns all across London firing at them, and puffs of smoke as the shells exploded. Then I heard the whistling sound of bombs falling from the sky.

"Right, inside!" snapped the warden, dragging me into the shelter. He pushed the heavy steel blast door shut as the bombs began to land – I could feel the floor shaking beneath my feet. "Phew, that was a bit too close for comfort," the warden said.

I didn't care how close it had been. I was just

desperate to be with Mum and Mavis, even if it meant I had to dodge bombs to reach them. "Please, you have to let me out!" I said, making for the door. "I can't stay here – my mum will worry!"

"I'm sure she will, but there's not much I can do about that right now," the warden said firmly. "Listen, I won't be opening that door until this raid is over and the all clear sounds. If you feel like complaining, then write a letter to Hermann Göring."

Hermann Göring was the Nazi in charge of the *Luftwaffe* – I'd often seen him on the newsreels. I thought it was a really stupid thing for the warden to say even as a joke and I wanted to yell at him. But there was no point – there never is with grown-ups. So I turned away and stomped off down the narrow concrete stairs into the shelter.

It was the size of my classroom but full of shadows, the only light coming from a dim bulb in the ceiling. About thirty people sat on wooden benches round the walls and across the middle. Most were grown-ups, although a few young kids were sitting with their mums. Everybody looked worried. Some had brought their gas masks, which was odd. So far in the war the

Germans hadn't used poison gas and many people had given up carrying gas masks, although you were still supposed to.

An old lady moved so I could sit down, but she took no notice of me from then on. That was fine – I didn't want to talk. I was angry with the ARP warden for making me stay in the shelter and worried sick about Mum and Mavis. I could still hear the whistling of the bombs and the bangs of the explosions and feel the floor shaking even more. It all brought back memories of the long nights during the Blitz.

The people around me did what people had always done in the shelters. Some talked, chattering away to keep each other cheerful, or maybe just themselves. Others stayed busy, playing cards, reading or busily knitting like the old lady beside me. A few were quiet, fear on their faces. I felt sorry for the mums. They had to keep their kids happy and it wasn't long before the nippers were grizzling and crying.

The warden told us his name was Arthur Jones. He walked round making sure that everyone was all right and handed out mugs of tea from a big pot he brewed.

"Sorry I had to be tough with you, son," he said,

standing over me. "Your mum would have approved, though. She wouldn't have wanted you out there in all this, would she? And I'll bet your sister and her are safe in a shelter somewhere."

"I hope so," I said, crossing my fingers like Mum. My anger with the warden drained away. He was right, he'd only been doing his job and now he was trying to make me feel better. "How long do you think the raid will last?" I asked.

"Well, this isn't 1940," he said, glancing up at the ceiling. "We've got a lot more night fighters these days, the ack-ack guns are better at targeting and Jerry doesn't have anywhere near as many planes. I reckon we'll be out of here soon."

The bombing stopped after a few minutes and the world outside fell briefly silent. Then we heard the steady drone of the all clear and everybody headed back upstairs. Arthur pulled open the blast door and I was the first person to leave.

"Good luck, son," Arthur said as I went past him. "Take care out there."

"Thanks," I said, then ran off up the Waterloo Road as fast as I could go.

There was a lot of noise now, the clanging of fire engine bells and men shouting. At first I couldn't see any bomb damage, just the glow of fires in the distance and columns of smoke caught in the searchlights. Then I came to a part of the road where a lot of bombs must have fallen, half a dozen of them taking out a row of houses and a big old pub on a corner. A couple of the houses were burning, which meant the Germans had also dropped incendiaries – special bombs meant to start fires.

Firemen were battling the blazes, spraying huge amounts of water on them from long hoses. A couple of ambulances stood by and I could see that their crews were taking care of several wounded people. I didn't look too closely. I remembered from before that if you did you might see something horrible and I'll admit I'm squeamish about blood and gore. I'd caught a glimpse of some dead bodies after one of the last raids in 1941 – we'd been coming out of the Underground at Waterloo and some buildings nearby had been hit. Mum had quickly held her hand over my eyes, but what I'd seen had played on my mind for weeks afterwards and had given me nightmares.

I'd forgotten what it smelt like after a raid – a strange mixture of smoke and brick dust, with the added aroma of gas leaking from broken pipes. An even nastier whiff told me that a sewer had been blown open too.

I hurried past, relieved that the rest of Waterloo Road hadn't suffered. Not much further, I thought, and then I'd be safely at home with Mum and Mavis.

I turned the corner into the road that would lead me to Wellington Mansions – and skidded to a halt. My heart stopped and the world fell silent once more, or that's how it seemed to me, anyway. Our block must have taken a direct hit. One end of the building had collapsed into a heap of rubble, broken beams and glass. A thick cloud of dust and smoke hung over it like the fog that sometimes covers the city.

I don't know how long I stood there without moving. It felt like for ever. Our flat – our *home* – had been in that end of the block. Now it was gone, destroyed.

"You all right, sonny?" said a voice. "You shouldn't hang around here."

Suddenly the world filled with noise again.

I looked round and saw a fireman behind me, the light of the fires back down the road glinting off his tin helmet. He was older than the others I'd seen, so I guessed he was a commander. A fire engine stood in an open space, the only part of the courtyard that was left. His men were spraying water on to a fire in the rubble, the flames hissing as they went out.

"What ... what happened to the people here?" I said. I could feel tears prickling in my eyes, but I wanted to put on a brave face. "Have you found any ... any..."

"Any casualties?" he said. "No, we think they all got to the shelters in time. Oi, Reggie, you need more on the left—" he called out, hurrying towards his men.

I breathed a sigh of relief and thought what a fool I'd been to expect Mum and Mavis to stay in the flat! That would have been too dangerous, so of course they would have made for a shelter, almost certainly the Underground at Waterloo. So that's where I ran to next, expecting to meet them as they came up from below, wondering how I could tell them we'd been bombed out and didn't have a home any more.

I didn't see them in the street outside the Tube,

so I ran down the escalator to the platforms, thinking they hadn't come up yet. But it looked like most of the people who had taken shelter had left the station when the all clear sounded. A few families had stayed in case of a follow-up raid – the *Luftwaffe* could be sneaky like that. There was no sign of Mum or Mavis, though, and I soon ran back up to street level.

I stood outside the station for a while, thinking hard about what to do next. Mum must have headed for our flat after she'd come out of the Tube with Mavis – only to find that our block had been hit. Where would she have gone then? They would have gone back to Marge's house, of course! I set off running once more, feeling even more stupid than ever, telling myself that's where I should have gone first.

The streets seemed a little quieter as I got further from the station, although I could still hear flames crackling and people shouting in the distance. At last I turned the corner into Marge's street – and I saw with a shock that it had been hit as well. Half the houses on one side were heaps of rubble with smoke rising from them. Two fire engines and an ambulance blocked the road, the crews standing there silently.

On the pavement in front of them were three bodies covered by blankets.

CHAPTER

I knew what they were straightaway – I'd seen dead bodies under blankets before. They were lying in front of the rubble that had been Marge's house, so I was sure I knew who they were, too. I ran down the road towards them screaming "Mum! Mavis! Auntie Marge!" I crashed into the back of the ambulance driver who was standing there. I nearly knocked her over, but she managed to stay on her feet.

"Hey, watch it!" she cried, clearly startled. I tried to push past her, but she held on to me. She was wearing a dark uniform and a tin hat, her fair hair poking out from under it. She was quite young and made me think of Mrs Peters, Mavis's teacher. But she was grumpy as well and that reminded me more of Mrs Reynolds. "What in heaven's name are you up to?" she said.

Just then a fireman came over. He was tall, well-built and about the same age as Dad. "Did you live in this house, son?" he asked, putting a hand on my shoulder. "He was calling out names, maybe they're his family..." he added, speaking over my head to the ambulance driver. They exchanged one of those serious grown-up looks, and even in the dark, I could see their faces were suddenly full of sadness.

"No, but my Auntie Marge did," I said. It felt so strange to be talking about living in a house that had been blown to smithereens. But then my home no longer existed either. "I think my mum and sister might have been in there with her too..."

We all turned to look down at the three bodies lying on the pavement.

"There's one way to find out," said the ambulance driver, her voice more kindly now. "I mean, you don't have to identify them right at this moment if you're not up to it, we can arrange something later. But to be honest, it might be better for you to find out now..."

I tried to answer, but my own voice wouldn't work. So I nodded instead.

The ambulance driver slowly pulled back the blankets covering the first and second bodies to reveal their faces. My heart was pounding – but they were two women I didn't recognize, one elderly, the other quite young. Their faces were pale and covered in dust and there was no blood, so they might have been sleeping. At last the ambulance driver pulled back the third blanket and I had to quickly turn my eyes away.

"That's . . . that's my Auntie Marge," I said. Her face was pale and dusty too, and all the life and fun had gone from it. She was quiet and still and she wasn't really Auntie Marge any more.

I'm not quite sure what happened next. I know I felt sick and dizzy and I think my knees must have gone, because I nearly fell over. The fireman and the ambulance driver managed to catch me, though, and they helped me sit down on the kerb.

"Take some deep breaths," said the ambulance driver. "You've had a shock."

I did what she told me, but it didn't help. Even though the ambulance driver had covered her again, I could still see Marge's white face in my mind. For a moment I thought that perhaps this was a terrible nightmare, that I was actually at home in bed and that when I woke up everything would be fine. The raid wouldn't have happened, our flat and Marge's house wouldn't have been bombed, Marge would be alive. Then I realised I was only trying to fool myself and I burst into tears.

The fireman and the ambulance driver were very nice. They stayed with me and after a while I stopped crying. The ambulance driver gave me a clean white hankie to wipe my eyes, but I blew my nose in it as well, so she said I'd better keep it.

"Right, let's get you sorted out," said the fireman. "Where *do* you live, son?"

"In Wellington Mansions, off Waterloo Road," I said. "That's been hit too."

I explained what had happened after I'd left the Regal and how I'd been hoping to find Mum and

Mavis with Marge. The fireman and the ambulance driver listened, and then they gave each other one of those serious grown-up looks again. I knew what they were thinking – Mum and Mavis might be under the rubble that had been Marge's house. And if they were, then they were probably dead as well.

"Let's not give up on them yet," said the ambulance driver. "They might have taken shelter elsewhere, and even if they *were* here they might have got out alive."

"She's right," said the fireman. "We weren't the first crew on the scene, so we might not have spotted them. I'll go and ask if anyone from the other engine did."

It turned out someone *had* seen a mother with a child of about Mavis's age. They'd been spotted outside a bombed house, maybe even Marge's, although nobody was sure of that. But I didn't get to feel relieved for long – there was bad news as well.

"I'm sorry, but it seems they were both injured," said the fireman. "They were taken to hospital in another ambulance, probably to St Thomas's – that's nearest."

"Oh no, they would definitely have gone to King's,"

said the ambulance driver. "Unless that was hit, then they might have been sent much further out."

The fireman disagreed and the two of them started arguing. I knew they were only trying to help, but I wanted to scream at them to be quiet. Eventually I spoke up.

"Is there a way I can find out where they are?" I said. "Who could tell me?"

"Your best bet would be Southwark Police Station," said the ambulance driver. "They'll have an incident room there and they should be able to help you to—"

She didn't finish what she was saying, for there was a huge *BANG*, the sound of a bomb going off. It was close, a couple of streets away. We all ducked, then looked up in the direction of the explosion. Smoke and flames rose high above the roofs, but there were no German planes in the sky, so I realised it must have been a delayed-action bomb. That was another really sneaky thing the *Luftwaffe* often did – they dropped bombs that exploded quite some time after they hit the ground.

That usually caused a lot of panic, mostly because nobody knew when the next one might go off.

So now there was a lot of shouting, and soon one of the fire engines raced away to the scene of the explosion, its bells clanging. The ambulance driver had disappeared and I was standing there alone beside Auntie Marge and the other two dead people. I didn't want to leave Marge, but I knew I had no choice. I knelt beside her and thought of Marge stood in the doorway of her house, smiling and waving at me earlier that day. I wanted to remember her that way.

"I'm sorry, Marge, but I've got to find Mum and Mavis," I said, my eyes filling with tears. "I know you'd understand ... and I'm sure they'll take care of you."

Then I ran down the street, heading for Southwark Police Station. It was on Borough High Street and I wanted to get there as quickly as possible. I *had* to find out what had happened to Mum and Mavis. If they were the mother and daughter who had been pulled from the rubble in Marge's street, how badly had they been hurt? My mind was full of dark thoughts and dread. I just felt so guilty that I had forgotten to collect Mavis, too. I should have been with them.

Ten minutes later I reached the police station, a long, red-brick building, and went inside. I'd never been in a police station before, but I'd seen them in films, so I knew what to expect. Beyond the doors was a room with a counter across the far end and a policeman – the desk sergeant – standing behind it. He was a big man, but his hair was grey and he looked like a granddad. There weren't many young coppers these days – a lot of them had been called up into the Forces.

A crowd of people stood at the counter trying to get the Sergeant's attention. "All right, all right!" he yelled, clearly losing his patience. "I can only talk to you one at a time! Now, it will be much easier if you show me your identity cards first."

I stood at the back of the crowd, wondering what to do. Then a door to one side of the counter opened and a lady came out. I knew she was in the Women's Voluntary Service because she was wearing the WVS uniform – a dark-green dress with a badge on the chest and a smart beret. She was as old as the sergeant, but she was small and round with dark hair, which made me think of Marge and that made me start crying again. I must have caught the WVS lady's attention because she came over.

"Oh dear," she said, smiling. "What seems to be the problem, young man?"

"I'm looking for my mum and sister," I said. "I couldn't find them after the air raid, but I think they've been hurt and I saw my Auntie Marge and she was. . ."

I couldn't say any more, but she seemed to understand. "Not to worry," she said, putting an arm round my shoulders. "I'm sure I can help. Come along."

She took me through another door, down a corridor and deeper into the police station. We eventually came to a door with a sign over it that said 'Incident Inquiry Point'. Beyond that was a room where more WVS ladies were sitting at desks, talking on phones or writing. A big map of Southwark covered one wall and yet another WVS lady was sticking red pins into it – the places hit by bombs, I guessed.

The WVS lady who found me was called Mrs Hamilton. She was quite posh and very brisk – she sat me on a chair in front of her and within minutes she'd got all my details written on a form. "I'm sorry to hear about your aunt," she said. "We'll do our best to reunite you with your mother and sister, but I'm afraid we haven't had any lists of casualties from the hospitals yet, so I can't tell you where they are."

"Can't I just go to the hospitals?" I said. "The fireman and the ambulance driver told me they'd either be in St Thomas's or King's and neither are that far."

"Oh no, I'm afraid that's not possible," said Mrs Hamilton, shaking her head. "I'll arrange a placement for you tonight and then we'll see about foster care."

"You mean living with another family?" I said, horrified. "How long for?"

"That rather depends on your mother's condition," said Mrs Hamilton. "It sounds like we'll have to find you and your family somewhere else to live and that could take a long time. You'll definitely have to stay in foster care till then."

She said a lot more, but I'd stopped listening. I didn't want to be separated from Mum and Mavis for days or weeks. I was desperate to find them *now* and I decided I should get out while I still could. So I jumped up and made for the door.

"I say, wait—" Mrs Hamilton called out. But I ran into the corridor and for the second time that night I crashed into someone, a policeman holding a boy by the arm. The boy was struggling, trying to free himself. When I bumped into the policeman, he lost his balance and his grip on the boy and fell to the floor. The boy looked as if he couldn't believe his luck and grinned at me.

"Thanks, mate!" he said. "Come on, let's scarper before he's back on his feet!"

The boy ran off and I stood there hesitating for a second.

Then I followed him into the night.

CHAPTER

I could barely keep up with him as he shot out of the police station and along the street. It was late now, past ten o'clock, and a bomber's moon cast a strange silvery light over everything – that's what people had called a full moon during the Blitz, because it meant the *Luftwaffe* bomber pilots could see the city better. There was a frost as well, the pavement was glittering and my breath was like a cloud in the cold air.

After a while the boy ducked into an alley and I followed. He turned into another, narrower alley, then another, and then he stopped, thank goodness. We stood there panting, both out of breath, but he was still grinning. I hadn't looked at him properly till now. He was small and skinny, his black hair shaved off on the sides of his head and sticking up on top like a brush. He was wearing a ragged jacket with patches on the elbows and dark trousers that stopped a couple of inches above his ankles.

"Thanks again, mate," he said. "I was in trouble till you showed up and sent that dozy copper flying! Pretty nifty, if you ask me. The name's Eric, by the way."

"What?" I said, confused. "Oh, my name's Jimmy. I didn't mean to do that to the policeman, it was an accident. I didn't see him when I ran out of that room."

"Really?" Eric said, but then he shrugged. "Oh well, it's all the same to me – I'm just glad we escaped. What did the old rozzers have you in for, anyway?"

I knew 'rozzers' was a slang word for the police, but I thought 'have you in for?' was a peculiar thing to say. I'd gone to the police station because I'd wanted to – did he think they'd *made* me go there for some reason? But then I shrugged too and told myself I was being daft. Eric probably just had a funny way of talking.

"I was trying to find out where my mum and sister are," I said. "I think they were wounded in the raid and taken to a hospital, but I don't know which one."

I felt tearful again, but I managed to hold it in this time. Eric seemed friendly, though, so I told him what had happened to me, spilling out everything as we stood there, the moon shining down on us.

"Blimey, you've had it rough, ain't you?" Eric looked quite impressed. "Have you got anywhere to stay tonight? Any other family to go to?" I shook my head. "Right, you'd better come with me, then," he said. "You need to talk to Frankie."

He shot off once more and I followed him again. I didn't have any choice – I couldn't think of anyone else to turn to and he seemed sure this Frankie could help me, whoever he might be. I wondered if Frankie was his big brother or a grown-up, maybe a friend of his parents. But I couldn't ask Eric about him – he kept running, down more alleys and across streets I didn't recognize, until I felt totally lost.

Eventually we came to a bombsite, a space where several bombed houses had been sealed off behind a tall fence of wooden panels. The authorities often did that if the houses were too badly damaged to be lived in or repaired. Some bombsites had actually been sealed off since the Blitz and the fences usually had 'DANGER! KEEP OUT!' painted on them in big red letters.

Eric, however, clearly wasn't bothered by the warnings on this particular fence. There was a small gap between two of the panels and he made it wider by pushing one inwards. "In you go," he said, and I squeezed through. Eric came in after me, and then led me across a stretch of bumpy ground to the houses. They were mostly rubble, but the back half of one still stood, with five steps leading down to a cellar door.

Beyond it were more steps and they took us deeper into the cellar itself. It was big with a high ceiling and reminded me of the Public Shelter I'd been in earlier. But there were no grown-ups in this cellar, just a dozen kids. The only light was coming from a couple of storm lanterns hanging from the ceiling and a few candles scattered on a long table in the middle. A small iron stove stood against the back wall, its door half open, with a warm red glow inside.

The kids stopped whatever they were doing and turned to stare at me. I was surprised to see them in there and I stared right back. There was an equal number of girls and boys. I realised they were of all different ages, a few of them quite young, some my age and the rest a bit older. Their clothes looked worn-out, but I'm sure you could say the same of almost everybody's clothes by that stage in the war.

A girl stepped forward, the others making way for her. She was taller than me, but I reckoned we were probably about the same age. Her fair hair hung to just below her ears and she was wearing a flowery-patterned dress with a tatty old brown cardigan over it and big, clumpy boots. She had green eyes, and she looked me up and down like I was something nasty she would have to scrape off the sole of her shoe.

"Who's this, Eric?" she said. "I thought I told you, no more waifs and strays."

"Sorry, Frankie," said Eric. "His name's Jimmy and he needs a bit of help."

"Oh, you're a girl," I said, unable to hide my surprise, and Frankie frowned.

"Blimey, he doesn't miss much, does he?" she said, and Eric sniggered. Frankie gave him a look and he instantly fell silent. "Were you expecting me *not* to be a girl, then?" she said, talking to me again. "What's Eric been saying about me?"

"Er ... just that you might be able to help," I mumbled. "So I thought—"

"So you thought I'd be a grown-up," she said, giving *me* a look now, the kind that's meant to put you in your place. "And not just a grown-up, a bloke too. Well, let me tell you, pal, you're lucky I'm neither of those things. It's the grown-ups who started this war, mostly the men, in fact, and they're the ones keeping it going."

"What are you on about?" I asked, suddenly feeling cross. "I didn't come here to listen to a load of rubbish! Eric said you might be able to help me find my mum and sister and I don't have time to hang around if you can't."

I turned to leave, but I didn't get far. "Whoa, hold your horses," said Frankie. "I didn't say I *wouldn't* help you, did I? What happened to your mum and sister?

You'd better come and sit down and tell me about it. Get him a chair, Eric."

I stared at her, all sorts of feelings boiling up inside me, wondering why I should bother. But then I thought I might as well find out if she had any ideas. Soon I was sitting on a wobbly chair telling my story for the third time that evening. I was almost getting used to going over it, so I didn't do any blubbing, although it was hard to hold it in when I told them about poor Marge.

Frankie sat in a battered armchair, listening. Eric and some of the others hung around, clearly curious, but most soon wandered off into the shadows.

I explained about ending up in the police station and talking to the WVS lady, Mrs Hamilton. Eric filled in the rest, telling Frankie that I'd knocked over the policeman and we'd made a run for it. "Hey, wait a minute," I said, "you make it sound as if I did that on purpose and you know I didn't, I told you. Actually, I'm beginning to think now I should just go back and say I'm sorry. Maybe the WVS lady got it wrong, maybe it won't take them so long to find out where my mum and sister are."

"Suit yourself," said Frankie. "But don't be too surprised if they drag you straight off to a cell as soon as you show your face in the police station. You knocked over a copper and that's a serious assault! There must have been loads of witnesses – and then you were seen running off with a known criminal."

"Oi!" said Eric, obviously offended. "I'll have you know I'm innocent."

"Pull the other one, Eric," said Frankie, laughing. "You were born guilty! It was only a question of time before you got caught. What had you been up to?"

"Nothing, I swear!" said Eric. "I mean, I did have a couple of tins of Spam in my pocket, but I didn't nick 'em from a shop like they said, I, er . . . found 'em. . ."

I began to feel sick as I listened. How could I have been so stupid again? Eric had been in the police station because they'd caught him stealing! And he'd thought I was there because they'd caught me doing something dodgy too. It looked like I'd managed to get myself into real trouble without even realising. I thought of Mum and what she would say. She would definitely be pretty cross with me.

"You all right?" Frankie said after a while, peering

at me and cutting into my thoughts. She seemed a little less unfriendly now. "You're looking a bit peaky. You're not going to pass out or anything, are you? Eric, fetch the boy a drink of water."

"I don't want a drink of water, thanks very much," I snapped, standing up. "In fact I don't want anything from you. I just want to get out of this ... *den of thieves!*"

I must have remembered that line from a film or a comic, I suppose. As far as I was concerned, it was the perfect way to describe the cellar and the kids in it. Frankie, however, didn't seem to agree. She jumped up and pushed me back against the wall till her face was only inches from mine. "Who do you think you are?" She said, jabbing a finger hard into my chest after each word. "I'm not having someone like you come here and call us names. You don't know the first thing about us."

"No, I don't," I said, shoving her off. "So how come you're here at this time of night, anyway? Do you actually *live* here? Where are your mums and dads?"

"They're long gone," said Frankie. "And yes, we *do* live here, and there are kids like us all over London.

Kids who were bombed out, put in foster homes they hated, then ran away. Kids whose mums were killed in raids and nobody could think of what to do with them because their dads are off fighting and they don't have any other family. We're just trying to survive and sometimes that means we have to bend the rules."

Frankie turned away and sat back down. I felt like a complete idiot – I seemed to have really put my foot in it. Even worse, I didn't know what to do next. I was desperate to track down Mum and Mavis, of course, but I wouldn't be able to if I was stuck in a prison cell, would I? Then I thought of Dad, and I realised that being in a cell would make it impossible to keep my promise to him too.

Suddenly I felt so tired. My eyes were sore and every part of me ached. I knew that what I really needed was a good sleep. Mum always said I got difficult and grumpy when I was over-tired. But I had a feeling I also needed some friends.

"Look, I'm sorry," I said. "Can we start again, please? I didn't understand until you explained all that. But now I think Eric definitely brought me to the right place."

Frankie stared at me, then shrugged. "Fair enough. In the morning we'll talk about finding your mum and sister. Put the kettle on, Eric. We could do with a cuppa."

But I was fast asleep before Eric could fill the teapot.

CHAPTER

I didn't know where I was when I woke up. I wondered why I was lying on a lumpy mattress under a couple of coats instead of being in my bed at home. I'd dreamed I was in that photo of Mum, Dad, Mavis and me in Margate, and somehow I felt I was still there with them. Then I heard Frankie and Eric talking and the dream vanished like a bubble popping.

They were sitting by the stove, both drinking tea from chipped mugs. The cellar door was open so some light was coming in and I saw that other mattresses were scattered round the room. But most of the kids seemed to have disappeared.

"Well, good morning, lazybones!" Frankie said, looking at me with a grin. "We thought you were going to sleep for ever. Come on, we've got a lot to do today."

She jumped up and pulled on a big old duffel coat, a bit like Dad's, then headed for the door. Eric followed her, but I didn't move. I still wasn't entirely sure that I was awake. "Er ... where are we going?" I said. "Can I have a cup of tea first?"

"Too late, you should have woken up sooner," she said, frowning at me. "And I'll explain on the way. Now, do you want to find your mum and sister or not?"

There was only one possible answer to that question. Once we were out on the street, Eric went off in one direction and Frankie headed in another. I had to walk fast to keep up with her and that was quite hard. I was still tired and now I realised I was hungry too. I also felt really grubby. Mum made Mavis and me have a wash and brush our teeth every morning and it seemed wrong that I hadn't done either.

It was a dull, overcast day, so I wasn't surprised to see there weren't many people about. Then I remembered it was Sunday, which was always quiet, mostly because everything was shut, of course. I actually felt quite cheerful – it was almost like I was on an adventure. I imagined I was William Brown from the *Just William* stories, and that Frankie, Eric and the others were The Outlaws. It was only a question of time before we found Mum and Mavis.

I soon began to recognize the streets again – I realised Frankie's hideout must have been somewhere near the Elephant and Castle. We passed a couple of bombsites where the Heavy Rescue Squad was working, skilled men digging through the rubble, checking for survivors. The smell of smoke, gas and sewage was everywhere. Some streets had even been sealed off, with signs warning of unexploded bombs.

We started walking up the Waterloo Road, heading towards the station. "Right, this is what's happening," said Frankie. "I'm going to speak to a few mates, put some feelers out, ask which hospitals last night's casualties were taken to. And I've sent Eric to talk to some other kids we know in the local foster homes.

That's where your sister might be if she wasn't hurt badly. Now, does all that sound like a good plan to you?"

"Er ... I suppose so..." I said. While she was talking, I'd seen two policemen on the other side of the road. They were on patrol, their faces stern under their tin helmets – just looking at them made me feel *so* guilty. I was sure they were about to spot me at any second and that then I'd be arrested. Frankie had seen them as well and she clearly didn't mess about. She took my arm and pulled me into an alley.

"Better safe than sorry," she whispered. "Let's wait till the coast is clear."

They went past eventually and we slipped back on to the street. I was beginning to feel faint with hunger, so I was relieved when Frankie said we should get something to eat. I'd forgotten that after air raids, the authorities used mobile canteens to provide free tea and sandwiches to anybody who'd been bombed out, as well as the firemen, the ambulance crews and the rescue squads.

We found one near the steps at the side entrance to Waterloo station, a large van with a long flap on the side that opened upwards. A couple of WVS ladies stood inside behind a counter, handing out sandwiches and tea from a big silver urn to a queue of people. I don't think I've ever eaten or drunk anything that tasted so good. I kept going back for more, but the WVS ladies didn't seem to mind.

Frankie had gone off to talk to somebody inside the station. When she returned, she collected a couple of sandwiches and a mug of tea from the van and we sat on the wide steps that led up to the entrance. Other people were sitting there too – half a dozen firemen with grimy faces and a couple of exhausted ambulance drivers.

"You were right," Frankie mumbled between mouthfuls of sandwich. "Some of the casualties were taken to St Thomas's and some to King's, but some were definitely taken to other hospitals as well. Nobody knows exactly where, though."

"Can't we just go and visit the likeliest hospitals?" I'd said the same thing to Mrs Hamilton, but I was hoping for a different answer this time. I didn't get one.

"You must be joking!" said Frankie. "If you're

asking after your mum and sister, you'll have to tell the nurses who you are and you gave your name to that WVS lady at the police station. You're probably on some kind of wanted list by now."

"Oh, right, I didn't think of that," I said, my heart sinking. A picture of a wanted poster popped into my mind, the kind you often saw in Westerns. But this time it was my face with the words 'WANTED, DEAD OR ALIVE' printed in big letters beneath it.

"Ah well, that's probably because you're not as clever as me," she said. "Come on, slowcoach, we've got a lot of ground to cover. I've barely even started yet."

She jumped to her feet and strode away and I followed. I soon found out she meant what she'd said. We walked for miles that day, up and down the streets of London, and Frankie seemed to know people everywhere. Some were kids and I guessed they were like her, living in a cellar, ducking and diving to get by. But she knew grown-ups too – most of them were all right, but some seemed very dodgy.

We even caught a bus into the West End – Frankie paid for the tickets. Mum had often taken Mavis and me to look in the shops on Oxford Street or Regent Street, and to get something to eat at a Lyons Corner House.

She talked to one bloke, who Mum would have called a 'spiv'. He was wearing a flashy striped suit with a double-breasted jacket, a fancy patterned tie and a sharp-looking brown hat. A thin line of bristles ran just above his top lip – a pencil moustache, as it's known. His name was Ronnie and when we bumped into him he was in an alley behind a pub, selling things to a small group of people, mostly tins of food, packets of tea, even a couple of bottles of American whiskey. Frankie waited until the other people drifted away, then asked the spiv if he knew where the casualties from last night's raid had been taken.

"No, sorry, Frankie," Ronnie said, shrugging his shoulders. "I'm not really interested in all that, to be honest. Although I suppose if old Adolf does start the Blitz again, then I won't have so many customers and that wouldn't suit me at all."

They talked for a long time, Ronnie telling Frankie what else he'd been selling recently. Most of it had probably been stolen, I thought. Everybody knew that was how the Black Market worked – dodgy geezers nicked things that other people wanted. They often stole from the Yanks – their Army had arrived in our country with mountains of supplies, so it wasn't surprising a lot of it went missing, especially food.

I didn't say a word while they were talking and I was glad when we moved on once more. I couldn't help thinking how cross Mum would be if she could see me with someone like that. I thought of Dad too, fighting the Nazis out at sea, and all the other sailors, soldiers, pilots and firemen who had been risking their lives last night. Loads of firemen had been killed in raids, not to mention ordinary people – like Auntie Marge.

But obviously somebody like Ronnie didn't care about them. He just thought of them as 'customers' and I didn't like that. In fact, by the time we started making our way back towards Frankie's hideout I was pretty fed up. I couldn't see the point of wandering around London talking to homeless kids and dodgy dealers. I was never going to find Mum and Mavis like that, was I? But I had no idea what else to do.

"Cheer up, misery guts," Frankie said, and slapped

me on the back. "We haven't found out much yet, but I bet we'll track your mum and sister down before long."

It was late afternoon by now, the sky growing dark. We were walking down a small street of shops near Mum's office in Whitehall. I thought of her lying in a hospital bed somewhere, maybe in pain, and I felt tearful again. I was angry with Frankie for wasting my time and for making me think she could help find Mum and Mavis. But suddenly the air raid sirens started howling and we heard the German bombers droning above us.

We weren't far from Westminster Tube station, although we only just made it there as the bombs began to fall. We hurried down the escalators with a crowd of people and found a spot on a platform, sitting on the floor with our backs to a wall. The bombs were much closer than when I'd been in the other shelter. One seemed to land almost on top of us and I felt Frankie shaking beside me. The anger I had felt vanished instantly. Frankie had seemed much tougher than me, but she was clearly terrified and I couldn't blame her for that. I was scared too.

"Are you all right, Frankie?" I said, taking her hand. "I'm sure we'll be safe."

"I'm fine," she said, although she didn't sound it. "I know we've got to be down here, but it always feels like we're sitting ducks, waiting for a direct hit. . ."

She kept talking, almost gabbling as the bombs fell, and I remembered Mum saying fear can make people do strange things. Well, being scared made Frankie talk, and talk and talk. Over the next hour I heard her whole life story, and what a sad tale it was. Her dodgy dad had left them a few years ago. Then her mum had got a new boyfriend, but Frankie hadn't got on with him, so she had run away.

Frankie told me Eric's story, and the stories of some of the kids in her hideout – they were all just as sad. I realised how lucky I was to have a mum and dad like mine – it seemed there were some bad grown-ups about. Then I thought of the grown-ups who had tried to help me – Arthur Jones the ARP man, the fireman and the ambulance driver, Mrs Hamilton the WVS lady. They hadn't seemed so bad.

Suddenly I knew what I had to do.

CHAPTER

This air raid was longer than the previous one and it was late when the all clear sounded. Frankie and me left the Tube station and ran across Westminster Bridge, the red flames of a fire further along the river reflected in the black water. The night was full of the sound of clanging bells, the yells of firemen and the smell of smoke. It took a while to get back to Frankie's cellar and I was glad when we did.

Eric was waiting for us and I could see he was pretty relieved when we turned up. I wasn't surprised to hear that he hadn't found out anything about Mavis. But that didn't matter now because I had a new plan. Soon everyone lay down to sleep and I decided to let them know about it in the morning, so they would have less time to tell me it was a stupid idea. But in the end it didn't work out that way.

I woke up before the others and realised I could get away without disturbing them, so I tiptoed to the door. But then I looked round at Frankie and Eric and the rest asleep under heaps of old coats and I felt guilty – after all, they had taken me in when I'd needed help. I thought of leaving them a note, but I didn't have any paper or a pen and I didn't want to hang about. So I decided I would try to help them somehow after I'd found Mum and Mavis. The truth is that they weren't like the kids in the *Just William* stories. What they were going through was real and it wasn't any fun.

A few moments later I was out on the street. It was Monday morning, the sky was grey and the air was chilly and smelt of smoke, but London was slowly coming to life. People were going to work and kids were heading to school, even if they had to clamber over heaps of rubble to get there. But I was making for somewhere else – Southwark Police Station. This time I wouldn't run away, whatever happened.

Mind you, I still stood outside for a while, getting the courage up to go in. I took a deep breath and went through the doors. The lobby wasn't as busy as it had been the other night, just a few people waiting quietly. I walked up to the counter and saw that the same desk sergeant was behind it. He's bound to remember me, I thought, my stomach tying itself in knots. I opened my mouth, but no words came out.

"Good morning, sonny," he said with a smile. "What can I do for you?"

"Er ... I'm looking for Mrs Hamilton, the WVS lady," I managed to say. "I need to speak to her..." I stopped talking and waited to be grabbed, but that didn't happen – the desk sergeant didn't recognize me! Suddenly I realised I'd been such a fool to listen to Frankie and worry so much. The police had probably forgotten about me the second I'd run out of the door. They *had* been pretty busy at the time.

"She's not usually here on Mondays," said the Desk Sergeant, and my heart sank. "But you're in luck –

she's come in today. I imagine she must have a lot to do after the raids this weekend. Through there, down the corridor, second door on the left."

It was the same room Mrs Hamilton had taken me to on the night of the raid, the one with the desks and the other WVS ladies and the map on the wall. Mrs Hamilton was frowning at a pile of papers on her desk, but she looked up as I walked in.

"Ah, Jimmy, isn't it?" she said, and raised an eyebrow. "You made quite an exit when you left the other night, young man. I'm surprised to see you again."

"I didn't mean to knock that policeman over," I said, wondering if I'd been too quick to think I'd got away with it. "It was an accident, honest, I swear. . ."

"Oh, don't worry, I knew that at the time," she said with a smile. "You should have looked where you were going, but you'd had a nasty shock and you were just keen to be with your mother and sister. Tell me, did you manage to find them in the end?"

"Actually, no, I didn't. So I was wondering – could you help me after all?"

"Why, of course I can!" she said, smiling even

more, her face lighting up. "That's what I joined the WVS for. Now I'm sure your form is here somewhere and I think those hospital casualty lists might have turned up."

I have to say that Mrs Hamilton was even more impressive than I thought she'd be. Once she got going there was no stopping her. She did have some casualty lists from the hospitals, but Mum and Mavis didn't appear on any. So Mrs Hamilton started telephoning the hospitals one after the other. It took quite a while, but she tracked Mum and Mavis down at last. They were in Lewisham Hospital.

"Well, Jimmy, I'm pleased to say that you can stop worrying," she said as she put down the receiver. "Your mother and sister are fine. They've got some cuts and bruises and it seems your mother has a concussion and a broken rib, too. The hospital kept them in as they were bombed out, mostly so they could get some rest."

Suddenly I felt a hundred times lighter. It was as if I'd been carrying a ten-ton weight around since the air raid and now it had gone. I should have been happy – but I burst into tears again. Mrs Hamilton came round from behind the desk, patted me on the shoulder and gave me her hankie. I blew my nose in it, so she said I'd better keep it. I put it in my pocket with the one the nice ambulance driver had given me.

I wanted to go to the hospital straightaway, but I'd never been to Lewisham and I didn't have a clue how to get there. It was all right though, because Mrs Hamilton said she would take me. We went by bus, we had to change several times, but we arrived eventually. The hospital was a maze of buildings and Mrs Hamilton led me into the largest one. The reception area was busy, but Mrs Hamilton spoke to another WVS lady at the information desk and she told us which ward Mum was in.

We walked down corridors that seemed to go on for ever, but we finally came to the right place. Mrs Hamilton pushed the doors open and I followed her through. The ward was a long room with a dozen beds on each side, all occupied by women. I soon spotted Mum – she was in a bed at the far end of the ward, with Mavis sitting beside her on a chair. I stopped for a moment, choking up, but then I ran to them.

I flung myself on the bed, hugging Mum. She hugged me and Mavis joined in.

"Oh Jimmy!" Mum said at last. She was crying, Mavis was holding on to me and crying, and of course I was blubbing away too. "I've been so worried!" Mum went on. "I asked them to find you for me, but you'd just vanished and I . . . I thought. . ."

"I know what you thought," I said hugging her harder. "I thought the same."

"Oww, Jimmy," she said, clearly in pain. "You'll have to stop squeezing me like that or I really will be a goner. You're not doing my cracked rib any good."

"Sorry, Mum," I said. I stood back and saw that she didn't look well. Her face was pale, almost as white as the hospital nightdress she was wearing and she had a bandage round her head. Mavis was also wearing a hospital nightdress and she was pale too. Her little face was bruised and scratched, and her right hand was bandaged.

"You all right, sis?" I asked. She nodded, and I ruffled her hair like Dad does.

"So where were you the other night?" Mum said, wincing as she made herself more comfortable.

"You didn't make it to Marge's when you were supposed to."

"No, you're right," I said. I thought about coming up with some excuse, some complicated explanation for why I hadn't gone to collect Mavis on time. But I knew that would be wrong, and besides, Mum always knows when I tell a lie.

So I told her the truth about everything I'd done since the last time we'd been together. She didn't look shocked when I told her that our flat had been destroyed – she already knew. The ambulance crew that had brought her and Mavis to the hospital had asked for our address and they'd recognized it immediately. Our block had been the first place to be hit and had been more damaged than any other building.

Mrs Hamilton had introduced herself to Mum and listened while I spoke. She looked very interested when I mentioned Frankie, Eric and the other kids.

Once I'd finished, Mum patted the bed and I sat beside her once more.

"You didn't do anything wrong, Jimmy," she said. "You should have remembered your sister, but that only rates a telling-off. How were you to know there was going to be an air raid? It surprised all of us. And as for staying with those kids and talking to a few spivs ... well, you could have got up to much worse things than that."

"So I'm not in trouble, then?" I said. "I didn't think you'd ever forgive me."

"For what?" Mum said. "I'm just glad you're alive. I'll admit I was cross with you when I got home and realised you'd forgotten about Mavis. I went round to Marge's and the three of us left the house when the sirens started. Marge was going to take Mavis to the Tube while I looked for you, but then she went back inside for her coat. Mavis and me were hit by the blast and we're lucky we weren't killed too."

Mum started crying again and so did Mavis and I. One of the nurses organised some tea and biscuits for us. After a while we stopped crying, but we were still glum. In fact, I didn't think I'd ever seen Mum looking quite so down. I remember thinking it was like being in the blackout – everything seemed dark and gloomy for us.

"I want to be practical with you now, if I may, Mrs Wilson," said Mrs Hamilton.

The nurses had given her a chair and she got a clipboard out of her bag. "You and Mavis should be ready to leave hospital in a day or two and I wondered if there was anywhere you could go – do you have any other relatives in London, for instance? Some friends you could stay with until we can get you properly rehoused?"

"No, there's nobody," said Mum. I could see her eyes beginning to fill with tears again. "We've got friends, but I doubt any of them would have room. And what about poor Marge? We need to sort out a funeral for her, and tell Alf, wherever he is."

"Don't worry, I can do all that," said Mrs Hamilton. "But finding somewhere for the three of you to live together might prove rather more tricky. There was a shortage of decent housing stock and accommodation in London before the war and the bombing has only made that worse. I'm afraid we might have to split you up."

"Definitely not!" I said, my voice loud enough to make everyone in the ward stare at us. Mrs Hamilton seemed startled and I thought I'd gone too far. "Sorry," I added. "I mean, we've only just found each other and we really don't want to be apart."

I looked at Mrs Hamilton across the bed, fixing my eyes on hers. I remembered a story in a comic about a boy who could hypnotise people and make them do what he wanted, and I wished I had the same power. But it turned out I didn't need it.

"I understand perfectly," said Mrs Hamilton with a sad smile. "I have a husband and three grown sons, all of them in the Army, and I would give anything for us to be together once more. I can't promise anything, but let me see what I can do."

I felt *so* relieved and I gave her my biggest smile. I was sure we could rely on good old Mrs Hamilton and that soon our troubles would be behind us.

There was still a very long way to go yet, though.

CHAPTER

They let me stay in the hospital that night. Dinner was a Woolton pie – they don't have any meat in them, just vegetables. Me and Mavis ate with Mum, the three of us sitting on her bed. Mavis had a bed in a children's ward, but the other beds were occupied so the nurses made one up for me in a store cupboard. I didn't mind – it was quite cosy and I was so tired I could probably have slept anywhere.

The nurses had also found me some pyjamas and they gave me a brand new toothbrush and some toothpaste. I had a wash in a bathroom near the ward and I felt much cleaner. I had to wear the same clothes again, though, and they were pretty dirty. Mavis said I looked just like Worzel Gummidge, the scarecrow in her favourite book, so I could tell she was feeling like her old self again.

There hadn't been another raid during the night, which was a relief for everyone. But I was still worried about Mum. She really did seem very low and she wasn't even trying to put a brave face on it, which wasn't like her. I worked hard at cheering her up, telling her jokes I'd heard at school and chattering away about anything that popped into my head. But I couldn't seem to get through to her at all.

The morning passed, we had lunch – watery vegetable soup and some disgusting fish paste sandwiches – and the afternoon slowly crawled by as well. I had begun to think that Mrs Hamilton would never come back. Then, at last, she turned up.

"Well, it wasn't easy and I had to pull a few strings," she said, her face serious. Mum and Mavis and me were sitting silently on Mum's bed, staring at Mrs Hamilton, holding our breath. "But I *have* managed to secure a flat for the three of you."

I cheered loud enough to make everyone in the ward stare at us once more, but this time Mrs Hamilton laughed. Mavis was pleased and Mum smiled faintly. But I knew she was still feeling very low and that somehow I would have to keep her going.

Amazingly enough the new flat was in Murphy Street, just round the corner from Lambeth North Tube station. It wasn't far from our old flat or our school, so we wouldn't have to get used to living in a whole new district. I liked having a Tube station nearby – we could get to it quickly if there were any more air raids. I had a nasty feeling rotten old Hitler hadn't finished with us yet.

The flat was on the first floor of a house in a long terrace. It had a couple of small bedrooms, a sitting room half the size of our old one and a tiny scullery we had to use as a kitchen. Everything was grubby and there wasn't much furniture, just an ancient table, some chairs and a couple of rickety beds. Worst of all, there was no inside toilet – we would have to use the one in the little backyard outside.

Mrs Hamilton helped us move in, although that wasn't hard. We didn't have anything but the clothes we stood up in and a bag with some food, tea and milk that Mrs Hamilton had bought for us. Everything else was still under the ruins of Wellington Mansions. We went past our old house on the bus with Mrs Hamilton. The rubble hadn't been fenced off yet and Mum said she couldn't bear to look at it.

Her mood didn't improve at the new flat. "I'm grateful for what you've done, Mrs Hamilton, of course I am," she said quietly as she looked round the rooms. "But we can't live here until I've given it a good clean, and I'm simply not up to it. . ."

"Relax, Mum," I said. "*I'll* do the cleaning. You won't have to do a thing."

"And I'll help!" said Mavis. "I can't let him have all the fun now, can I?"

"That's the spirit!" said Mrs Hamilton, beaming. "What lovely children you have, Mrs Wilson. I'm sure this will soon be a proper home for the three of you."

In the morning me and Mavis got stuck into the cleaning, under Mum's guidance, of course, and over the next few days the flat began to look better.

Mrs Hamilton found us more furniture – a settee, a sideboard and even a half-decent wireless like our old one – and arranged for it all to be delivered. She said it came from bomb-damaged houses, but it wasn't too bad. She also got Mum some money from the government and she sorted out new ration books and identity cards for us.

Mum's friends from work came round as soon as she let them know where we were. They helped us with more clothes, food and anything else they could think of. Mum contacted Mr Jackson at St Edmund's and he paid us a visit as well. Mrs Reynolds came with him and, to be honest, I was dreading seeing her. But I have to say Mrs Reynolds was completely different away from school and she couldn't have been nicer. Mr Jackson said Mavis and me didn't have to go back to school till we felt up to it.

It wasn't all plain sailing, though, as Dad would have said. For a start, Mum had to decide what to tell Dad – she didn't like the idea of him being worried while he was at sea. I said we should let him know what had happened, but also that we were fine now. Besides, he needed our new address, otherwise he wouldn't know where to find us when he next came home on leave. So she wrote all of that in a letter. Then she had to write another letter to Alf, Marge's husband, and that was much harder.

Mrs Hamilton posted the letter and she also found out about Marge's funeral for us. Marge had been taken to St Thomas's, and Mrs Hamilton got in touch with her family – she had a mum and dad and a couple of older married sisters. They arranged for Marge to be buried in Camberwell Cemetery, a week after we'd moved into the new flat. Mrs Hamilton gave them our new address and they invited us to the funeral.

It was a cold, windy day, and a very sad one too. There were lots of tears in the chapel and even more when Marge's coffin was lowered into her grave. Afterwards, Mum stayed to talk to Marge's family and Mavis – who was upset by the whole thing – clung to her. But Mrs Hamilton had been invited too and I went over to speak to her before she left. Something had been really playing on my mind.

"Er … excuse me, Mrs Hamilton?" I said. "I've been thinking about Frankie, Eric and the other kids. I was wondering if you could help them somehow."

"Of course I will, Jimmy," said Mrs Hamilton. "It's shameful nobody has helped them before. Beating the Nazis is important, but it's no good if we miss the bad things happening right under our noses. Just tell me where they're living."

I didn't know the address of Frankie's cellar, so I gave Mrs Hamilton directions and hoped she would find it. If anyone could sort things out for Frankie and the other kids, then she could. Frankie would probably be cross when she found out what I'd done, but that didn't matter. I just knew it was the right thing to do. I also had a feeling that deep down Frankie didn't want to live that way anymore either.

CHAPTER

Time passed and the war dragged on. There were lots more air raids and everyone started talking about it being the 'Baby Blitz'. It wasn't as bad as the proper Blitz, but it was still pretty scary when the bombs were falling. Mum found it hard to deal with, because of what she and Mavis had gone through. We took shelter in Lambeth North Tube station, but she didn't even feel we were really safe down there.

Mind you, the war was beginning to go badly at last for rotten old Hitler. Every night on the BBC

News Alvar Liddell told us what was happening. The Nazis were on the run in Russia, and the RAF and the Yanks were bombing their cities. I have to say I felt pleased when I heard that, but then I felt a bit guilty too. I realised a lot of ordinary people – like poor Marge – were probably getting killed in German cities.

Things were going better at sea, too – it seemed the Royal Navy was winning the Battle of the Atlantic, as Alvar Liddell called it. Of course it was, I thought. How could it be otherwise with men like my dad and his mates fighting the Germans? Dad hadn't replied to Mum's letter yet. It often took him a long time to reply when the *Defiant* was out at sea. I kept telling Mum that, but I knew she was worried.

Mrs Hamilton kept in touch. She popped round from time to time to see how we were getting on. It was always good to see her, and one day she brought news of Frankie. It seemed she'd gone to Frankie's hideout and said she'd like to help them, and Frankie had quite liked the idea. In fact, I realised that Mrs Hamilton and Frankie would probably get on very well – they were both good at organising things.

So I decided that I could stop worrying about Frankie, Eric and the others.

Mavis and I went back to school after a while and Mum went back to work when her rib felt better. I volunteered to leave school early every day so Mavis and me could come home together – Mr Jackson and Mrs Reynolds said that was fine.

"All right, Jimmy?" said Harry on that first morning. We were in the playground, waiting to go inside, shivering in the cold. "Here, I've got something for you."

He handed me a bundle of comics, old editions of *The Beano*, *The Wizard* and a few others too. Then he dug deep into the pocket of his short trousers and pulled out a bundle of trading cards – the ones I'd given him and a load more.

"I don't get it," I said, surprised. "Why are you giving me these? I've nothing to swap."

"That doesn't matter," Harry murmured, looking embarrassed. "You've had a rough time and I just wanted to cheer you up. Is there anything else I can do?"

"Thanks, Harry, that means a lot," I said.

"Actually, now you mention it, can you come with me somewhere on Saturday?"

I'd been planning this particular outing for ages. I wanted to visit what was left of Wellington Mansions to see if I could find any of our stuff. On Saturday morning I asked Mum if I could go round to Harry's house. For a moment I thought she was going to say no – she liked us all to be together just in case there was a raid. But I begged and pleaded and promised I wouldn't be out long and she gave in.

It was a cold, wet March day and there weren't many people about. What was left of Wellington Mansions had finally been fenced off, but it was easy to get in. It felt strange being back and for a moment I was even a bit tearful. But I kept myself under control and got on with what we'd come to do. We clambered all over the rubble, searching everywhere, but we didn't find much and I began to think it was a waste of time. Then at last I caught a glimpse of something sticking up between some broken bricks. I gently pulled it out and I could hardly believe what I'd found – it was the photograph of Mum, Dad, Mavis and me at Margate! The glass was cracked and the frame was a bit wonky, but you could still see us clearly.

"I think this will do, Harry," I said grinning at him. "I don't need anything else."

"Fair enough," said Harry, smiling back. "Well that ought to cheer up your mum!"

We said goodbye and went our separate ways. I hurried home, hoping he was right.

"Mum, you'll never guess what—" I said as I opened the front door and went in.

Mum and Mavis were in the sitting room and they turned to look at me. I could tell they'd been crying, but they were smiling happily too. That seemed strange – I hadn't seen Mum that cheerful for a long time. Suddenly I realised what it must mean.

"Hello, son!" said a deep voice behind me. "You're just in time for a cuppa."

I whipped round and saw Dad in the scullery doorway, still in his uniform. Behind him the kettle was on the hob and the teapot and cups were all set out and ready.

"Dad!" I cried. I hugged him as hard as I could and he hugged me back.

He explained that he had been given special leave from the *Defiant* because of what had happened to us. He didn't have long with us though, just a few days.

"What's that you've got there?" he said at last, taking the picture. He held it up and looked at it for a moment, then showed Mum and Mavis. "Blimey," Dad said. "That seems like a long time ago, doesn't it? We've been through a lot since then."

"But we're still alive, aren't we?" said Mum. "We're bruised and battered like the picture, but we're not beaten yet. We're going to win this war too, I'm sure of it."

I just wished rotten old Hitler could have been there to listen to her. After all, Mum was *always* right.

HISTORICAL NOTE:

THE PEOPLE

Jimmy and his family are fictitious, but their experiences are based on historical accounts of people who experienced life in London during the Second World War.

EVACUEES

In 1939, hundreds of thousands of children were evacuated from London and other cities around Britain. However, when the expected bombing raids on cities failed to materialise, many parents whose children had been evacuated decided to bring them home again. By January 1940 almost half of the evacuees returned home.

Children who came back to London often had nowhere to go and nothing to do. Schools were closed, teachers were evacuated, dads were called up, mums had to work, so the children fended for themselves – and often got into trouble.

TIMELINE

1933
After years of struggle following World War One, the Germans vote for Adolf Hitler, leader of the Nazi party, because he promises to make Germany powerful again.

1939
SEPTEMBER – Hitler invades Poland on 1 September. Britain evacuates children from cities. Britain and France (the Allies) declare war on Germany on 3 September.

1940
JANUARY – rationing begins in Britain.

APRIL – Germany invades Norway and Denmark.

MAY – Germany invades Belgium, France, Luxembourg and the Netherlands. Churchill becomes British Prime Minister. Allied troops are rescued from the beaches at Dunkirk.

JUNE – Italy joins the war on Germany's side.

JULY – the Royal Air Force defends Britain against attacks by Nazi Germany's air force, the *Luftwaffe*. It becomes known as the Battle of Britain.

SEPTEMBER – the Blitz begins and the *Luftwaffe* continues to bomb Britain until 1941.

1941
JUNE – Hitler's armies begin the invasion of Russia.

AUGUST – the German siege of Leningrad begins. It lasts for 872 days.

DECEMBER – Japan attacks Pearl Harbour. The United States enters the war on the Allies' side.

1942

NOVEMBER – Germany suffers defeats at Stalingrad, Russia and El Alamein, North Africa.

1943

FEBRUARY – German defeat at Stalingrad.

MAY – German and Italian troops surrender in North Africa.

SEPTEMBER – the Allies invade Italy.

1944

JANUARY – the *Luftwaffe* attacks targets cities in Britain. This attack becomes known as the 'Baby Blitz' and continues until May 1944.

JUNE – the Allies launch the D-Day landings in Normandy, France. The first German V1 rocket attack on London.

AUGUST – the Resistance uprising, Paris is freed from the Nazis.

1945

APRIL – the Soviet army advances on Berlin. Hitler dies in his bunker.

MAY – German troops surrender to the Allies. 8 May Victory in Europe (VE Day).

AUGUST – the United States drops atomic bombs on Hiroshima and Nagasaki. Japan surrenders on 14 August. The war is over.

LEADERS DURING WORLD WAR TWO:

The Allies:

WINSTON CHURCHILL – British Prime Minister from 1940

FRANKLIN D ROOSEVELT – US President until his death in April 1945

JOSEPH STALIN – leader of the Soviet Union

GENERAL BERNARD MONTGOMERY – commanded Allies in the D-Day landings

GENERAL DWIGHT EISENHOWER – commanded US troops in Europe and Africa

GENERAL GEORGI ZHUKOV – Russian commander who seized Berlin in 1945

The Axis powers:
ADOLF HITLER – Germany's dictator

BENITO MUSSOLINI – Italy's dictator

EMPEROR HIROHITO – ruler of Japan

ERWIN ROMMEL – Nazi General known as the 'Desert Fox'

HERMANN GÖRING – Commander of the *Luftwaffe*

GLOSSARY

ARP Air Raid Precautions

ATS The Auxiliary Territorial Service, the women's branch of the British Army.

BLITZ The German word for 'lightning'. Originally used by the Nazis in the phrase 'Blitzkrieg' or 'lightning war' to describe their tactic of using tanks and aircraft in mass attacks. 'Blitz' quickly became the word used to describe the bombing attacks on Britain in 1940 and 1941.

HMS Stands for His/Her Majesty's Ship, always used before the name of a ship in the Royal Navy. In World War Two the monarch was King George VI.

KIWI A slang word for New Zealanders – a Kiwi is a flightless bird native to New Zealand.

WAAF The Women's Auxiliary Air Force.

WRNS The Women's Royal Naval Service, usually known as 'Wrens'.

YANK A slang word for Americans.

AUTHOR'S NOTE:

Both my parents lived in London during the Second World War – my mum was thirteen when it began and my dad fourteen. My mum was evacuated, but soon came back to London and experienced the Blitz. When she was old enough she joined the Women's Royal Naval Service, the 'Wrens' and my dad joined the Navy. He served on HMS *Belfast* and saw action in the North Atlantic and on Arctic Convoys to Russia. They met at the great Naval base in Portsmouth and got married in 1946.

While I was growing up, I heard lots of stories about what life was like in London during the war. Families were separated from each other – children were evacuated and fathers called up and sent off to fight. Mothers definitely didn't have an easy time of it, though. They had to work long hours in factories and offices, doing all the jobs that men had done before the war – and look after their children as well. Then there was the rationing, the endless bad news and constant air raids.

We tend to think of the Second World War as a heroic struggle against evil, and in many ways that's true. Adolf Hitler and his Nazis did terrible things and had to be stopped, and millions of ordinary people played their part in the war very bravely. But some people took advantage of the chaos caused by the war. There was plenty of crime, which was understandable. There were lots of shortages and the government was concentrating most of its efforts on trying to beat Hitler before he beat us.

The chaos affected everything, including schools, as we saw in the story. My mum and dad always said they didn't get much education at all once the war started. There were plenty of real Frankies and Erics – children who ended up having to look after themselves in one way or another. It took a long time and a lot of effort by people such as Mrs Hamilton to sort out the problem. Even after the war there were still gangs of children getting into trouble, in London and other British cities.

Yet people – and families – survived. Jimmy and his family and all the millions of people like them didn't know – even in 1944 – that Nazi Germany would eventually be defeated. But they still carried on – doing whatever they had to, sticking together and helping each other through everything that Hitler could throw at them. And that's one of the reasons I wanted to write this story. For me, in many ways they were just as brave as the soldiers, sailors and airmen who were doing the actual fighting.

Just like my mum and dad, they deserve to be remembered too.

JIM ELDRIDGE

1918

COMING HOME

A FASCINATING FIRST-HAND ACCOUNT OF ONE OF THE MOST DANGEROUS TIMES IN HISTORY

CATHERINE JOHNSON

1783

FREEDOM

A GRIPPING FIRST-HAND ACCOUNT FROM A CHILD STRUGGLING TO OVERCOME ADVERSITY